RANDOLPH LAD

DNA Raiders- An Explosion of Trumps

First published by Radolph Lad 2023

This novel is entirely a work of fiction. The names, characters and incidents portrayed in it are the work of the author's imagination. Any resemblance to actual persons, living or dead, events or localities is entirely coincidental.

Randolph Lad asserts the moral right to be identified as the author of this work.

First edition

This book was professionally typeset on Reedsy.
Find out more at reedsy.com

Contents

Foreword — v

A Picture of Trump — vi

1 Chapter 1 — 1

2 Chapter 2 — 4

3 Chapter 3 — 6

4 Chapter 4 — 8

5 Chapter 5 — 10

6 Chapter 6 — 12

7 Chapter 7 — 14

8 Chapter 8 — 16

9 Chapter 9 — 18

10 Chapter 10 — 21

11 Chapter 11 — 24

12 Chapter 12 — 27

13 Chapter 13 — 30

14 Chapter 14 — 33

15 Chapter 15 — 35

16 Chapter 16 — 37

17 Chapter 17 — 39

18 Chapter 18 — 41

19 Chapter 19 — 43

20 Chapter 20 — 45

21 Chapter 21 — 47

22 Chapter 22 — 49

23 Chapter 23 — 51

24 Chapter 24 — 52

25 Chapter 25   53

26 Chapter 26   58

27 Chapter 27   60

Final Words   63

Foreword

If you read Elvis Leaves the Lab you noticed it was short and sweet, it was a small look into the world of DNA Raiders, just a taste. This book is a full banquet, It fleshes out a lot of the supporting characters. It paints a bigger picture , on how the DNA Raiders do what they do.It brings the world into a brighter understanding.

I hope it paints a picture in your mind you can understand.

Thank You
Randolph Lad

A Picture of Trump

1

Chapter 1

This one will be different, no one copy of a famous person created but five, another thing no extra programming or training involved. Easy maybe, but that's never guaranteed, not in this line of work. Another strange aspect of this job it wouldn't be for a wealthy person but a group of scientists who want to do research.

Dr. Daniel hoped this deal wouldn't cause him any headaches. His last one had left a sour taste in his mouth, and his pockets a little light. He needed to put that all behind him, and close the door to that deal. It would be draining to keep old wounds open, he needed to move on, so he could concentrate on the business at hand.

Donald Trump, a sad tragic little man of the past would be Daniels next creation but as five separate clones delivered as babies, each one raised in a different environment to test the age old question was it nature or nurture that created a persons soul, that made a person who and what they are.

Creating five separate copies of the same person, would be the easy part. Plus getting Trump DNA wouldn't be a hard task, he left it all over the place, and Mar-A-Lagos was still under his family name and under their control. A trip to Florida for Trix was in order. She would visit the mausoleum of Trump that in most part had been turned into a memorial and museum in his name.

Daniel went to the office that was Trix's sanctuary. Trix was a strange bird that had strange habits.You never could know what mood she would be in.Her emotions were not stable in any sense of the word.Daniel fingers in his mind were crossed.

Daniel entered a room that looked like the world biggest hoarder lived there. Trix was not a person who was a clean freak.This room sure looked it. Daniel found a chair to sit after he moved of spilling papers from it.

But Trix always caught her man,or at least the man's DNA.So far she never failed, a perfect one hundred score.So Danial had no worries about the outcome of this case.It would be easy, peasy as Trix always said.

"Got a new one for you Trix", Daniel said as he sat in his shaky, not sure if it was safe chair.

"How easy", Trix reflected back as she starred at her computer screen seeming to not be paying attention.
     But Daniel knew looks could be deceiving , he knew Trix could and would remember everything said.
     So he continued, "Remember a former president named Donald Trump" .
     Trix said." vaguely, but not really,why"?

"We need his DNA,should for you be an easy in and out grab"Daniel smiled.

Ok,"She said". I'll get on the internet,make all the set ups, Suppose I'll need to fly to ,where Daniel"?
     "Florida, you can get some sun and get out of this room".

" Hey", Trix who felt maybe a little bit embarrassed said,"What's wrong with my room".

Daniel just laughed shook his head " It's your place to got to live in it".

Trix made a face,and got to work. She was a fast typist it wouldn't take long,to get everything ready to roll.

2

Chapter 2

Trix got her old tin can of a car started,with the money she was paid she could of gotten one that wasn't a lemon. But when asked by her fellow coworkers she said," I like lemonade". No one bothered to ask anymore. It wasn't much of a trip getting to the airport. So she knew it would get her there,once there she would park it in the lot, and it would be there when she got back. No one was desperate enough to steal this pile of crap.

She found a spot in the parking lot,that had a few empty spots near it,didn't need any new dents on her baby,it didn't need anymore character.It had plenty.She looked for someone to help her with her bags,she wasn't a muscle bound strongman. She wasn't totally helpless,but all her gear would break the camels back.She saw someone pushing an empty cart, she waved a hand and scream in here loudest voice"hey I could use some help here".It worked she thanked god.

The man pushing the card didn't look like someone filled with a lot of energy.In fact he looked down right lazy.In Trix's mind she was saying," I saw my grandma of ninety move faster using a walker". But she kept a smile on her face,glad she at least got some help.

It took awhile to get in the airport, but she was lucky she knew the rules,always get there early ingrained into over years of travel,she was no newbie.She was a veteran of air travel,she won her stripes.At clearing the entrance her head turned to scan the area. She was the kind of person who noticed everything.Her mom when she was a child gave her the nickname Eagle Eye.She rarely missed anything.

She navigated the crowded airport like a prize bullfighter navigated a bull fight,She bumped into no one and no one bumped into her.She would of been a great bullfighter.In the distance she saw her destination,the counter she needed to get her ticket,and then get ready to get on her flight.Hoping all would go well,she wouldn't get stuck near a crying baby,or an passenger who wouldn't shut up.

3

Chapter 3

Well she got lucky this time.No crying babies, no loud drunks,and the plane arrived when it was supposed to. She had like every time she flew read a book. it wasn't a long flight from New York to Florida so she got a few chapters in and it was a relaxing trip.

She left the plane, she was glad to be on land again.Flying wasn't her favorite thing to do. Nope, not. She would have to rent a car,but nothing she could rent would make her feel as safe as her old clunker left behind in New York.She would miss old Betsy,the name she gave all of her cars since she first drove.She would find something not to fancy, fancy cars did nothing to her heart.Something simple would do.

The clerk at the car rental desk looked young and perky.Trix didn't do perky.She made a frown as she got to the front of the short small line. "I need a car",she said,"something cheap,but reliable,something that will get we where I need to go".The girl smiled as she rattled off names of cars,until Trix heard one she liked. " I'll take the Oldsmobile". Trix thought not a fancy choice,but a dependable one.

She loved the car because it didn't have that new car smell,it instead smelled like a car that's been around the block a time or two. She started it and it purred like a happy kitten.A Smile came across her face,so far so good

The job was going good, but this wasn't Trix's first rodeo,evidently Murphy would pop up and something would go wrong.It never failed.

4

Chapter 4

The trip to the hotel she chose as her home base,wasn't far from the airport,or her target destination Mar-A-Logo. She had chosen the best,most efficient place possibly to get the job done. That was one of Trix's gifts.Her office might look like it was hit by a tornado or two, but once on a job she became a model of efficiency.

The desk clerk after a few seconds recognized Trix in front of her."How can I help you". Trix gave a simple reply,"I have a reservation for a deluxe room". Trix liked an old car,but wasn't allergic to pampering herself when it came to hotel rooms. The girl looked at the computer screen."here it is right here,would you need help bringing up your bag". Trix knowing she had more gear than she could carry. "sure".

An old man came with a cart,loaded up the cart with Trix's gear,"There you go" Trix said,"thank you".They went to an elevator ,waiting till it arrived. Once the door opened the man pushed the cart into the elevator.Trix then entered.When it got to the right floor, Trix got out. Then the man with the cart got out and said,"This way mam". Trix nodded her head in reply and followed.

Once in side the room,Trix pulled out a $10 bill,said "thank you". as the man unloaded the cart next to the bed in the room, she gave him the tip.

The old man looked past the retirement age,she knew how that worked with the way the world was not many people could afford retirement and were forced to work till the day they died.

5

Chapter 5

She got out a map of the area, she was a very thorough planner. Her cases were planned out like a military invasion. All the T's were crossed,nothing left to chance.She noted how far away the final destination was,and in her mind calculated how long it would take to get there. She than pulled out a complete blue prints of Mar-A-Lago. She decided what would be the most efficient places to search as she thought of what items might hold the target DNA. She weighed all the possibilities in her mind and by what she knew about Donald Trump,hair DNA would be the best bet.

Once the planning was done,she put the gear together she would need to get it done.She didn't carry a gun,if it came to that she already failed.She didn't mind using mace, or even a shock stick.Killing someone would be a step to far,a hill to far to climb. Killing someone would open a big can of worms that would end up ending the whole show. Game Over.

This time she would carry her own gear,this time she needed to keep everything she did a secret.A show no one but her would see,and no one not even her boss would hear the complete story.That's the way Trix worked,that how she kept her value.She had made herself invaluable like a beautiful diamond,but one with fangs.She always got her DNA,she has never failed once.

The car she rented was there ready and waiting. It's dull shine catching Trix's eyes as she neared.She placed her hand on the door and did a silent prayer in her head,"come on baby lets get this done".She opened the door got in,adjusted the seat,and the mirror. She took a deep breath to set her in motion, turned the key. Away we go.

6

Chapter 6

Once she got to her destination her minds focus turned on to full control.Her mind started processing everything around her like it was a super computer.Everything became crystal clear and motion slowed down.,She was in the zone.

She wouldn't be going in the front door,she would use a service entrance off the kitchen.She pulled car over and parked not right at Mar-A-Lago but close enough to be in easy walking distance.She had made sure to dress in a way that didn't stand out so that she was bland that she wouldn't create a strong memory if anyone saw her.She had her plain Jane costume on as she called it. Finally to act like she belonged there, she after doing this job for so long she did on autopilot.

She got to a door on the back side of the building. She pulled the handle,Locked. Lucky for her locks were toys and she was able to open any one.She got out the tools she had in one of her pockets and quickly unlocked the door. Opening it slowly while listening for sounds within she heard nothing.She went in looked around noticing nothing that would stop her.She took a breath,counted to five and continued on.

Trump bedroom or the bedroom that used to be Trump bedroom since he been dead for awhile was her destination. There had to be a piece of Trump hair there, and once she found it, tested it, she could be on her way.

It was persevered as a shrine to the late president Donald Trump, a shrine only the people at the time of it's creation had been important.It had long ago lost in shine,No one remembered a one time mediocre man who was president. The novelty wore off quickly not long after his death.

She at first of course looked for brushes and combs, then checked his pillows and bed. She had a device that contained a vacuum that she ran over many surfaces.Once DNA was found it would set off a buzzing alarm. The she would have to test it against a bloodline sample with another device. If it was a match, she would put it in a container to transport it back to New York.

It took a hour before she struck gold,a few false alarms but in the end like always she got her DNA. Trump would be signed,sealed,and delivered. Dr Daniel could get to work.

7

Chapter 7

After a day of travel Trix arrived back at the hub.As soon as she entered the hidden tunnel she made her way to Dr. Daniel office. After she entered she threw a break-proof container at an open Doctors hand.

Then she smiled and said"I got it"

Daniel a person with a drawn on poker face who rarely smiled shrugged and replied," of course you did I never thought you wouldn't".

Daniel could move the project to the next stage, Creating five clones of Donald Trump. He went to his lab that had to be kept super sterile so no stay DNA could get introduced to the clone creation. If that happened it could end up in something not even close to being human created. Humans with say a spiders DNA could be dangerous. So even before entering the creation room he would have to go through a decontamination chamber, ever bacteria and bug would get erased from his body. Once through that he would don a decontamination suit. Protocol must always be followed or bad things can happen.Joe, Dr Daniels only assistance would have everything prepped and ready to go. For this work he had a special microscope that could easily see the DNA. This time for this project he would replicate the DNA, he would at least need one cells worth for each of the five embryo's he would need to create. He added the chemicals that would quickly make the DNA replicate.

14

After 20 minutes he would start the separation process picking the five best cells and putting them in a prepared egg. Once that happened each one of the five eggs would be put in a separate growth chamber. Since they wanted a baby it would be ready in two days.Since they also wanted a blank slate, no programming or training would be required

8

Chapter 8

Two days have passed since the embryo's were placed in the growth chamber.They did what they do, and are all the size of a new born baby, five identical babies. Each one would be taken from the chamber and sent to five very different families. One rich, One poor, one middle class, one African American ,one Chinese American. Daniel thought about the Scientist and the experiment they were researching he thought "interesting". What would win nature or nurture? Daniel if he was a betting money he would but it on nurture.

The first baby was wrapped in a warm blanket and placed in an infant car seat. It was to be taken to a wealthy New York address,it would be the so called control and would be raised like the actual Donald Trump had been raised. That would mean by a nanny mostly,then on to various boarding school. Not much parental contact.

The second baby was wrapped in a warm blanket and placed in an infant car seat. It would be taken to a poor family in New Jersey. It would be raised in a poor household that lived on public assistance and only survived through help. One thing though is that it would be a loving home. Where plenty of time would be spent on the babies care.

The third baby was wrapped in a warm blanket and placed in an infant car seat. It would be taken to a middle class family that lived in Pittsburgh. It would be raised in a household where both parents worked. Maybe for the first three months the mother figure would be there, then babysitters would take over,then daycare. Then school in a public school.The child would have some contact with it's parents but it would be limited.

The fourth baby was wrapped in a warm blanket and placed in an infant car seat It would go to an African American Family living in Cincinnati . It would live in a family of modest means,but one that was large and had many relatives.The child would be most likely treated with racism, and it would need to grow up strong to survive.

The last and final baby was wrapped in a warm blanket but this time it was taken on a airplane. This delivery wasn't in driving distance it was being taken San Francisco to live with a Chinese American Family. This family still lived by many of the old Chinese traditions. Education would be very important and baby Trump would be pressured to excel.

No one was told these babies were a clone of any kind. that would of prejudiced the results. No one knew little Trumps were their babies.

9

Chapter 9

The First baby arrived on the door step of the wealthy family named the Austins.It was a mansion in an exclusive gated community in upper state New York. It was massive and a little intimidating. Wealth at it's most gaudy .

The naming would be up to the Austins, They would have to make a choice it, but according to a contract each family signed it would need to be soon.Every scientific test needs a set of guardrails, they are imposed to create a somewhat even playing field. This family would be expected to live like a wealthy one. If whatever the baby wants or needs it was to be given without delay, the child was to be spoiled rotten like the original Donald Trump was.

The name was chosen

Carlson David Austin , ok that's a bit pretentious,but it was a name. Little Trump would have to learn to live up to it.

The next part of the agreement was that a complete record would need to be made. In this case that would most likely be the nanny at first, then someone at whatever private school they sent Carlson to would have to be paid to keep a record.

The baby was taken to the room that had been created, to be it's home until being sent to private school. The room , the nursery had every modern gadget at the time. Whatever could be automated would be.Rocking would happen whenever the baby cried, soft music would seemingly come from nowhere playing to sooth Carlson whenever needed. Bottles would be ready at the push of a button for the nanny to use.Diaper changing could be done quickly with no smells released this was some hi-tech stuff.

10

Chapter 10

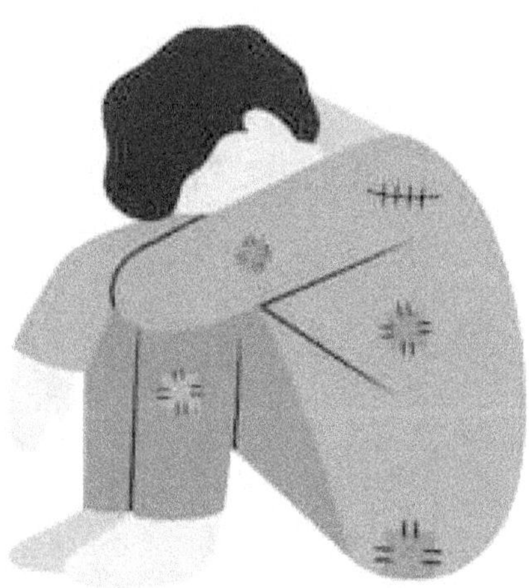

The next clone baby was taken to New Jersey a not pretty place there. A part of the state that had fallen on hard times. Many of the people who lived here barely scratched out a life. Many only lived through a life line provided by the government. Just enough to barely make it, just enough food to live, just enough medical care to live.Kids in many cases if there wasn't free breakfasts or lunches at school would starve to death. This Trump baby clone wouldn't live with a silver spoon in his mouth.

A simple name was chosen

Kiel Jacob Smith

The people chosen to be parents would do all the work, no babysitters here and no nanny. No money for those things. The future would be going to a public school in a depressed part of town.to a school that barely could keeps its doors open.

Kiel would be raised as cheaply as possibly everything done the old way. No hi-tech here. Old diapers that could be washed after each use, formula purchased through benefits from the WIC program. All medical care provided through benefits of the state. He would be raised like a poor child in a poor family

The parent would keep all the records in this case.

The father did odd jobs to keep the boat afloat,it would barely last the curves life threw but somehow it did.One thing they had was an open heart and life hadn't beat the kindness out of their soul.

11

Chapter 11

This Little Trump would go to a middle class family living in Pittsburgh. A modest home where the father made enough so the wife could stay home.Money would be saved for college for little Trump.It would be a white bread life,a life like a majority of the American people. A home of educated white people, who believed in hard work and that anyone who didn't work was lazy.

The name chosen for the third Trump Clone.

David Jones Keller

What would be expected of David. Lots would be expected, he would have chores,get an allowance, he would be expected to join a sport. He would be expected to have lots of friends,and do well in school.This was the idea middle class family, with middle class values.It was an open place to grow to your full potential.David would be tested and expected to pass with flying colors. College, then a good middle class job.His father would expect he be good in some sport. Be it basketball,football or baseball he would need to excel.

The baby room was decorated in blue, The rules would be followed blue for boys, pink for girls. Middle class families mostly lived by the rules set over the years. There was an expected way to live. Nice crib,changing table, and a sturdy rocking chair was placed in the room. Teddy bears were placed in various places in the room as an after thought. David would live a comfortable life here.But would be expected to contribute to the family in someway.As the father said ,"no one gets a free ride".

12

Chapter 12

This area was for a family of modest means in Cincinnati. It was a home on the average side of the spectrum.Nothing overly fancy but respectable. This would be the fourth baby in line.It would not look physically like the rest of the tribe. It would be a white baby,in a black American world. This dynamic would cause interesting problems, some would be unexpected and unique.Would reverse racism occur or not. Would he be bullied and how would he react to it.The Scientist who created the program think this child would produce some very interesting data.

Name

Samuel James Washington

He most likely will be called Sammy,by everyone around except maybe the teachers in school.His new father was a Doctor who worked in the local Hospital. His mother stayed at home but worked from there through the internet.It would be a comfortable life in someway, but maybe hard in others.Life has no guarantees, nothing is written in stone.Kay sirrah, sirrah , what will be will be. The futures not our to see. That song sums it up. That's why this experiment was being done in the first place.

This baby's room was filled with hand me downs, Sammy would have older siblings, he would not be an only child this time.His parents would be veterans of raising children.They wouldn't be in case of content anxiety,they would know what to do,and expect in almost every situation. No rushing a sick kid with a cold to the emergency room. Baby gets a cut, they will clean it and put a band aid on it. It would be over. None of the first child drama.

13

Chapter 13

This family was living In San Francisco, in a place called Little China. A baby raised here would be immersed in Chinese history and culture. Holidays would be celebrated, The older persons in the household taught the younger ones the history passed on from generation to generation. Households held the current living family tree, Grandparents, parents, and children all lived in one house.Each providing something in their own way.

The Name

Johnny Win Sung

The Johnny part to pay homage to his United States birth, the rest of the name to show his Chinese heritage.That was a tradition in Little China to always do things to remember where you come from.Some would always consider their homeland to be China. No matter how many generation never stepped foot there.

He would be expected like all Chinese American children to be head of their class, and always be the best students in class. He would have to study till everything taught was imprinted in his mind.Perfection was expected, perfection would be rewarded, and vice versa non perfection would be punished in some way. This was the Chinese way.

It was hard at first until perfection would be ingrained,and easier and easier to achieve. Once the system was perfected being perfect would be easy. Johnny like a sword would be tempered, made strong,made reliable.

14

Chapter 14

Carlton the early years. A private preschool to a private elementary school. Carlton was a bully, His privileged upbringing where he was treated like some prince created someone who thought everyone was beneath him. He didn't have friends he had followers, other children he could manipulate , ones who were weak and easy to control.

Carlton told a kid name Tony," go get me another pudding". Like some trained pet, Tony jumped up and ran off like some peon to do his masters biding. That was kind of sad. But Carlton didn't see it and if he did he didn't care. Only Thing he cared about was himself. The only emotions he had were negative ones. Love or the idea of love was foreign to this little boy with a big ego. He never really gotten any, his parent sure didn't show him any.

Elementary years went by with not much change, no real friends made, Carlton became a master of lies, a facade created by false myths. No one would ever know who the real Carlton is. He kept that hidden, locked up in his heart,never to see the light of day.He was a master puppeteer who stood in the shadows pulling the strings. He never committed acts that would end him up in the principal office, he had others, to take the risks ,while he would bathe in the glory of his revenges .

He took pleasure in the misfortunes of others. People he considered bugs, not humans.

At even this young age, he started to lie to create a false myth of who he was. He would put up a false front of greatness, He would claim he was great at everything and anything. He wasn't even close to that being true.

15

Chapter 15

Kiel was a good kid. He had nothing, but he had love. The people who were his parents actually loved him as if he was their own.He had plenty of friends in the neighborhood and at school. Everyone was in the same boat, everyone was poor. No one thought they were better, but equal in value.

It was an us against the world , world. We all had to cover each others back to get by. That's what happened here, it had to,or it would all come crashing down.Public school was a short bus trip from where Kiel lived. He would get up in the morning,get clean and dressed , Get on the bus,so he could get there early enough for breakfast at school.

The school he went to had seen better days, There was probably hidden health dangers in every wall. Asbestos check, lead paint check, air filters anywhere no check. This old school had been around for over a hundred years,and it wouldn't be replaced soon. It couldn't be afforded in this poverty ridden area. The city had no incentive to make it better.It could care less about what the poor thought or needed. They rarely vote.

Kiel was just one of the faceless crowd,he had decided a long time ago not to standout, he kept his head down and, did his class work, got average grades. He did just enough to not get noticed. He didn't want to be the shiny coin that stood out. He saw that as trouble.

The reports sent to the scientist would show he was an average student and an average poor child.

16

Chapter 16

David had draw the middle class straw. His adoptive father had started him in sports as early as possible. He went from T-ball to Peewee league in baseball. From flag football to youth league football. Even being part of a youth bowling league was squeezed in there somewhere.

He was expected to get good grades, because if he didn't well his sports would be cut. His father no way would let that happen.This father was living through his son, getting a high off his child victories on the fields of play.

David grew up in a pressure cooker, His father would yell his head off if he made even one bad grade. This turned him into a child whose emotions where always on edge. It got him into a few fight when his anger over his father needed an outlet. But his father would ignore that as long as he won the fight.

David had anger issues, the school was on the verge of recommending counseling . He would again have to bury his feelings or suffer his father wrath.Being middle class in some families meant certain standards had to met. A rat race of keeping up with the Jones,worrying about the future was the norm.

David was not a happy camper, his life was a constant hill he had to climb. They penalties for failing could be sever.

17

Chapter 17

Sammy at first had a hard time being a white boy ,in a black boy world, but that didn't last long.Having older brothers and sisters put a stop to that in a hurry. They learned to love the little white boy,and would risk their lives to protect him. School was hard in the beginning, but bullies aren't stupid and could learn things that would stop pain from coming their way. Picking on Sammy was one of those thing.

So he learned and grew,and was expected to do good. He would do it to make his parents and siblings proud, he felt like it was something he owed them.He had a safe and warm feeling every time he thought of his family.

Under the right conditions even the weakest flower responds and turn beautiful.All the right ingredients were present. Love in unending amounts,plus good friends,and a family that will support your dreams. Sammy was become a strong healthy boy, both mentally and physically.

He didn't have an once of hate,he did well in school,went to church every Sunday. It was the perfect soil to prosper in.He had many friends because he had a inviting personality, he was open,and honest. He was faithful,and loyal.He had all the qualities that made people good friends. Life long types of friends.

He wasn't old enough to notice girls, but he was getting there. He did have one girl where he felt an urge around,but that would need to grow maybe into love,or maybe into friendship? The future would decide that.

18

Chapter 18

The Little China part of San Francisco was always alive.There was all some kind of Chinese holiday being honored in someway. New Years, New Moon, Something for every season. Some how dragons were always involved , very colorful ones. Firework first created a long time ago in China,was something used in every holiday.

Today was a holiday,a time where perfection could be forgotten, at least for a little while.Holidays at school would be a time of fun,to celebrate and be happy, filled with joy.Today was one of the biggest to celebrate Chinese New Years. Johnny loved this time of year,he could for one day have his stresses lifted and just be a kid.

No perfection required,No sticks or carrots. Freedom from the trials of life. Life wasn't easy, it should not be one big vacation. Johnny had that idea burned into his brain on many occasions. He knew he had responsibilities to make his family proud. But for today that didn't matter.

Tomorrow would be different back to what was kind of a prison cell where the real Johnny was a ghost and a faded memory.But he knew that shadow well and could turn it on at the drop of a hat. All his homework was perfect,neat,clean and all done right down, to the last decimal point or period.

He was a lonely boy surrounded by people.That was his lot in life as it was.

42

19

Chapter 19

First Reports are in so far everything as the hypothesis saw it as happening. The Trump clone that was raised like the original was Turning out like the original. Carlson David Austin was a chip off the original block. Greedy, A person who had a over average size ego,and was someone who bullied anyone who challenged him in anyway. He in the reports was shown to not be a good person.

Kiel Jacob Smith was an exact polar opposite to Carlson. He was a breath of light,where Carlson was a dark storm cloud. Kiel brought goodness to the people around him,he brought love,and understanding. The people around him caught his sunshine and passed it on to others. He was a spreader of good vibes that spread wherever he went.

David Jones Keller was a jock.He had a muscular body built through a lot of hard work.He would let nothing stand in his way to get better. He had to be the best in whatever sport he competed in. The original Trump was never close to being an athlete of any kind.He never had the motivation to be that. David did and through all the pain, and the being so tired he could barely move, he attained his goal or should we say his father goal. To be a great athlete.

Samuel James Washington was a happy kid,He had a life surrounded by a large family of siblings, four older brothers, three older sisters. He was number eight, The last, the end of the line. Mrs. Washington was having no more babies. Tubes were tied,the birth machine was closed for business. Samuel got love from all directions , his sisters would treat him like a doll and add him to their play until they grew out of such things. His brothers when he got old enough would take him out to play sandlot baseball or out to build a fort in some long abandoned lot. Of course there was a neighborhood basketball courts where teens would start games to set the pecking order on who was the best hoops master.Samuel was growing up in a balanced way.

Johnny Win Sung was an "A" student. Only thing that could happen, He went to the mental boot camp his family created. "A,s" are the only thing that was allowed. Failure was not an option. It was a mentally hard life, It was a drain most days, others it was even worse. Scientist doing the study had no prediction on where this one was going. The possibilities Johnny crashes and burns out.He survives it all and become a genius who does something to change the world. The saying there is a fine line between genius and insanity may apply

It was the half way part and the experiment would continue till the clones reached eighteen. But even after then reports would come in through the total life of the clones.

20

Chapter 20

High school in this Private School was divided into cliques that were based on if your family was old money or new money. If your family were billionaires or millionaires.Carlson was in the billionaire family group.He had a fast car he droves to school that cost close to a million dollars.His clothing were bought in the finest stores. Everything about him screamed wealth.

His cliques was him being the leader,because his ego would except nothing less. He could never be a follower,not of anyone. How did he get there to being leader? He stab so called friends in the back. Threw others under the bus. He did that until he was the king of the hill.His heart was a black unused organ that's only job was to beat.

It was an all boys school, So it was filled with boys who had nothing to do with their hormones. So any chance for any sex with a girl was taken advantage of. Even if they had to buy it. David learned about girls by paying for sex.He learned the birds & the bees in a way that had nothing to do with love. To him girls were there only to be used to fulfill his sexual needs. That in the end will lead to a lonely life.

No serious relationships ever found. Not in the places he was looking.Friends would only be fair weather ones until he lost all his families wealth.True friendships were none existent. It was a dog eat dog world, survival of the richest.

After school he was now being groomed to take over the family business.He was expected to learn from his father, how to be a business man.Who knows if these lessons would be able to break past the barrier of someone who thought they knew everything.Not long till graduation and a full time job in the family business.

He knew he would have passing grades, he paid the smartest kids enough to do his homework and as for tests he had a so far undetected way of cheating.

21

Chapter 21

Kiel's high school years were great until one fatal case of being in the wrong place and at the wrong time. Shots rang out and after the shooting was over the body of a young teen was found. Kiel became just another victim of the streets where poor people live. He wasn't the first and most likely won't e the last. Nothing changes

He had a bright future, he had enough smarts to maybe go to college. Those dreams became nightmares with one act of senseless violence. Kiel had become his parents whole life.A big empty whole had been torn in that. It was one big sad ending to a promising future. It wasn't fair but no can guarantee a fair life.

The broken body was loaded in to a ambulance sitting by the curb,the lights creating a shifting kaleidoscope of colors, and shadows.There was no hurry, no rush, no matter how long it took nothing would change. Pictures would need to be taken by crime scene photographers,evidence would have to be picked up and bagged. The coroner would have to come to the scene and collect the body,and fill out a death certificate.

The autopsy would need to be done, so the report could be used in court if the person who killed Kiel was ever found. All the evidence collect will hopefully end up in someone being held accountable but that doesn't happen in half the cases. Not in a big city where murders happen every week and police resources are stretched to the breaking point.

Chances were not good. The body of Kiel was released to the funeral home that would get him ready for his final trip in a cold coffin to a poor part of a local cemetery. No money for a fancy stone, a small marker would show his resting place. The cheapest funeral allowed that would mark Kiel's once living spirit in passing.

22

Chapter 22

David was I guess was living the middle class dream or maybe his father was. David had to make First string,in football, basketball, and be the pitcher in baseball. His high school life was map out by his father, no detours from the path would be tolerated. It would end up with him getting a sports scholarship to a top ten sports program school.

But life has a few bumps in its path and a big one could sink the whole dream. David got his girlfriend pregnant.This could derail the whole train. David was not ready to be a father ,not for a long time. Davids dad was furious, that he would screw up this badly, and put his future at stake.Plans where made that the girl would get a abortion, but the problem of her being a Catholic put that one out the window. She would be sent away to have the baby in a place in another state where a relative lived. Hopefully she would have the baby ,put it up for adoption and come back to her old life,with no one the wiser.

David took her to the bus station. He claimed he would wait and he would always love her. Even as he said it he knew it was an empty promise his father would never let him keep. Tears were shed and he would probably never see her again.

He would finish High School, get a scholarship and never look back. He wanted out.That's what happened he got a scholarship to Notre Dame, he would be a fighting Irish. After that he still had dreams of going to the NFL.

23

Chapter 23

Sammy sailed through High School with flying colors, He was on his way he decided to become a doctor. He wanted his doctor dad to be proud of him following him in his foot steps. None of the other children did and Sammy knew it pulled at his fathers heart. He decided he would be the one to fulfill his fathers dream of a being doctor.

The plan, first a good college with a quality pre-med program. Four years of that, then a quality medical school. Finally a residency at a good teaching hospital. He would try to go to the schools his dad did and end up doing his residency at the same hospital. He loved helping people, this job as a doctor would be a good fit.

But all plans don't work as written he could go to the college his father did, but he went to another. He did go to the same medical school, but no open residency were available at the time he needed one. So he found one at another hospital. He knew he would need to put the time in,he heard his fathers horror stories over the years. Nothing worthwhile is easy, he knew that lesson well.

24

Chapter 24

Johnny's high school years went by in a blur. No drama slowed him down,He would finish high school, find a college, study business and come back to Little China, He would take some of the work off his parents shoulders, so they could slowly retire over ten years. Then the business would be his.

Meanwhile his mother was playing matchmaker something all Chinese mothers took as a duty. Johnny had no time to look for a girlfriend, he always had his head in a book. But one girl his mother introduced him to did catch his eye. All future dates would be chaperoned, it was a little old fashion, but old fashion was a part of Little China.

They went to a movie, but sitting behind the couple was the girls brother.They went to a restaurant but sitting in the table just next to them was the girls sister. Every date there was one of the girls family within speaking distance.After awhile Johnny tuned them out, put at first it caused him a little shyness. Overtime that disappeared as he became more comfortable with the girl.

It didn't take long for love to bloom. Future plans between the families were already being decided. Everyone knew in the end Sunny the girl would marry Johnny the boy.

25

Chapter 25

Eighteen years have gone by.

The final results would be collected and analyzed . It would be gone over by each scientist on the team of seven.Each writing there conclusions. Then they would discuss those reports and it would then be decided what would be in the final report.

Dr. Janus Reed, Had A PHD in Sociology , basically that means she studied how society worked to shape peoples thoughts and reactions. Her report would be from that scientific view point.

Janus was a little said when she heard Kiel didn't survive the experiment, he was one of the more interesting subjects. But it wouldn't stop the project, but add to it by understanding economic factors,Violence in poor areas, and other factors related to poverty.

Everything in total would add more data,good or bad,to the report and it's conclusions .Janus went over all the reports, and in her opinion nurture was the factor on how a person became who they are. It was clear as day

---

Dr Bob Landon, Had A PHD in Psychiatry he studied the thought processes of the mind and how people created what we would call their personalities. From that view he would look for what motivated people to do what they do.

There are patterns in everything, and everywhere. Bob was looking for those patterns in the data. What made the subjects mad, what made they sad,what made happy ,what made they afraid.what made them bold. Each emotion would tell a story,leading to a whole picture.

After all he research, he would have to also choose nurture. Only one of the Trump clones came close to being like the original. The one raised in the almost same conditions.

Dr. Roy St. James, Had a PHD in Genetics, He would be looking how the brain reacted chemically, and genetically to stress . One thing never mentioned before is that each child had a special medical exam each year of their lives, where genetic samples were taken. Roy study that data,that was his job, to check hormone levels, and anything that would effect genetic changes and growth.

What surprised him that there where any differences at all being it was really the same person but just in separate bodies. But overtime there was like a divergence of each one become uniquely different in a different way. Somehow they started to become genetically different. As time passed the difference became more visible. This was a very not an expected result. He came up with the conclusion that nurturing changed the actual physical make up of the subjects.

Dr. Larry Samson his PHD was in Racial Sciences, How different Races reactive in similar situations. That what he would look for in the data. Three of the subject were raised in white persons home. One Wealthy, one poor, one middle class. They other two subjects were raised in a different race home. One African America in an upper middle class setting, the other in a Chinese American home that was lower middle class.

How did race effect the subjects? What ideas were given to the subjects by their racial involvements?How was their belief system created? What racial components contributed to their character growth.

First the highest score of being a racist was easy to see was the wealthy Trump Clone. The second highest The Middle class Trump. The least racist was the poor Trump Clone. The other two Trump clones had a slight racism against white people. Larry was not surprised this went along with all previous data on race that he knew.

That there were differences proved racism was a learned thing, That supports the concept of nurture

———

Dr. Sidney Blaine, Had A PHD in Religious Sciences. That was the study of how religion effects society. Each Subject would be looked at on how religion effected them.Rich Trump wasn't a big going to church person, he rarely set foot in one. Sadly poor Trump didn't either because they couldn't afford to. But that doesn't mean no religion. Religious values were taught to him by his parents. Middle Class Trump did go to church every Sunday, but it was more something done out of habit.Not much actual religion was making it into his brain. The African American subject went to a baptist church weekly, and was also involved in our church activities.He had the strongest faith and knowledge of Christianity. The Chinese American Subject was in a Buddhist family, and was actually very religious in that religion. With all that it looked like being religious needed to be nurtured

——

Dr. Clive Redden, Had a PHD in Parentolgy , That was a rather new science that studied the different styles of parenting. Wealthy Trump had limited contact with his parents. he was raised by a nanny in infant hood , and wasn't long before he was sent to live at a private school. So he kind of gained a habit of doing anything to get attention from his parents and from the world. So he created in himself a grand ego, and used puffery and lies to make himself seem bigger than life.He knew everything and could do anything, not really but that didn't stop him from making those claims.

The poor Trump even though they lived by modest mean, never did not feel love. He felt like somebody cared and would be there if he faltered in life. He had a great support system.

Middle class Trump was driven by a father who was trying to live his dreams through his son. The son was mostly at first was forced into sports. After time it became a habit that he would play sports.He no longer questions it, and it became a personal goal. The years of mental abuse did it's work, the getting yelled at, or holding back of praise whenever he wasn't falling the so called program,and every time he won getting gifts and praises. Training in him a pattern of actions that he would live with for the rest of his life

.Africa American Trump had a good family model , creating his behavior. Lots of siblings created a special bond that could never be broken.His parent were strict but also very loving. It was the perfect way to teach him responsibly, He learned that lesson well. His future looked very bright

Chinese American Trump was raised in a structure family that lived by traditions. Every thing was planned without many surprises. It was tough at times, but it created a tough subject who learned how to handle anything threw in his way.He would go to college ,marry the girl his mother chose for him. He would one day take over the family business when his parents grew to old.

Again Nurture was the force that built the clones character

____

Dr. John T Waddle, had a PHD in Economic Science, He would report on how economic factors effected the subjects.

The wealthy Trump clone was given everything and anything he wanted, there were zero limits set.

The poor Trump clone got very little of anything. Only the essentials were provided

The Middle Class Trump had limits set to his performance in sports. If he did well he got want he wanted, if he failed as a penalty he would be denied.

The African America Trump was expected to work in someway to get things.He was taught a work ethic.

The Chinese American Trump was basically the same as the African American Trump with one added item, grades that were good were rewarded, but bad grades were punished by holding back on things wanted.

How did this effect the subjects Wealthy Trump was more original Trump like, The poor Trump was the least Trump Like, The Middle Class Trump had some original Trump characteristics that were minor, Final both the African American, and Chinese Trumps had only slight amount of original Trump characteristics.

This would prove Nurture was the controlling factor that was in effect here.

26

Chapter 26

Final Report

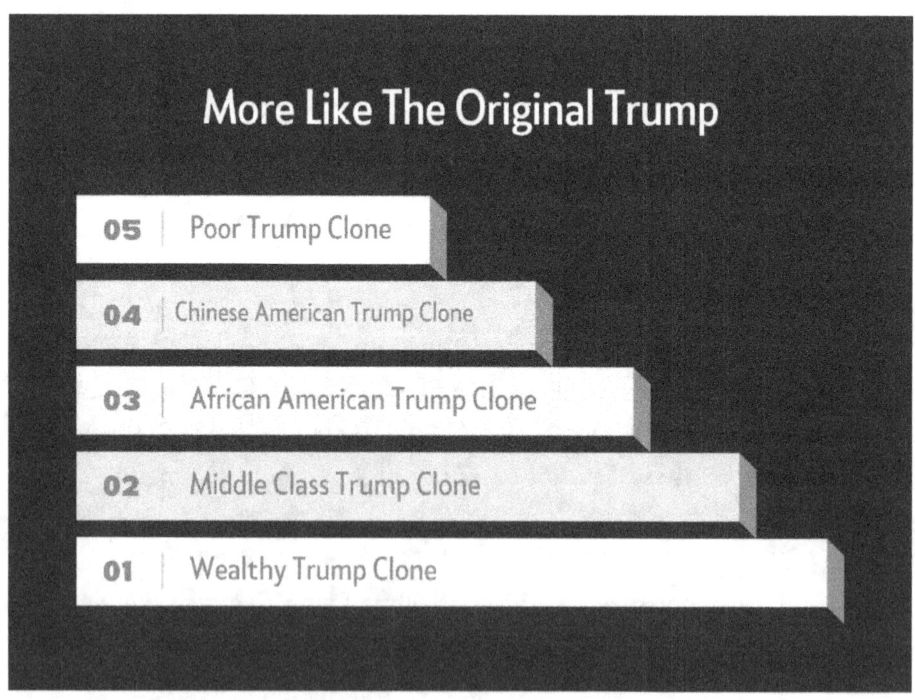

Graph of what study showed, Who was more like the original.

Wealthy Trump Most Like The Original

Middle Class Trump had some of the originals characteristic

African America and Chinese American Trumps were statistically similar and had a few Original Trump characteristic.

Final the poor Trump had no similarities with the Original Trump.

____

The final report with all the contributions by all the scientist , with all their education in the various sciences came up with the same conclusions. Nurture was the main factor in creating a persons character. The condition people are raised under make them who they are and will always be. It's what was expected 18 years ago when the experiment was created and now in this case it was proven. But of course all things in science need to be replicated in future experiments. So in no way is this an end but a beginning.

Chapter 27

Carlson David Austin lived a long life. He was caught up in many scandals,lived a life of always trying to stay one step from the law catching unto his illegal activities. His thought of being above the law, would be his undoing.

____

Kiel Jacob Smiths- His life was cut short. It could of been good for the world if he lived, he was the most likely to effect the world in a positive way. We will never know what could of been

____

David Jones Keller would never make it as a professional Athlete , One tragic accident in one college game ended any possibility for a future career in professional sports. His dad took it harder than David himself. He would end back in Pittsburgh, his so called glory days behind him.He would go on to be a Realtor selling houses to others.

____

Samuel James Washington Became a doctor who saved many lives in his long career. A brain surgeon at the local hospital ,his father once worked his magic in. He had gotten married, had created his own large brood of children,and like him in his generation one had decided to follow in his foot steps. He died surround by family at a ripe old age.

———

Johnny Win Sung , married the girl his mother chose for him.He actually was very in love with her. He did end up running the family business and it prospered under his care.One of his children will in the future be made the new owner when Johnny decided to retire and move on. That would follow the family tradition first started many generations ago.

———

Final Words

During those 18 years time didn't stand idle. At the headquarters of the DNA Raiders countless other clones were created for other clients. The wheel keeps turning. Change chugs forward on the track of life. Dr. Daniel would be kept busy, because who didn't want a celebrity clone slave. Catch Future book.

This book followed some science, but some were totally made up to push the story. So do not use this all as some fact in science. It's not , I tried to make it logical as possible, but even though, some of it is conjecture and not based on any actual facts.

Remember this is science fiction, remember any science fiction story has some elements that might not be connected to actual current facts.That doesn't mean that a science fiction idea can't become science fact in the future.

Look at the stuff Jules Verne put out there that was fiction at the time that later became science fact.

Who knows where anything can land in a future world.

Randolph Lad